King
Oak

Edited and designed by Fern Flynn and Bob Ogley

© Ron Denney and Bob Murray 1989

Published by Froglets Publications

Brasted Chart,

Westerham, Kent TN16 1LY

Telephone 0959 62972

ISBN 1-872337-00-7

Jacket design by Alison Stammers.

Printed by Staples Printers Rochester Limited, Love Lane, Rochester, Kent.

Part of the proceeds from the sale of this book will support the restoration of Knole Park.

Mr. Murray's watercolours are available as prints on request to the publishers

# of Sevenoaks

A story of our time

by Ron Denney Illustrations by Bob Murray

THE old trees stood proudly at the top of the hill leading into the town. They were the seven oaks and the town bore their name. They stood like sentinels round a famous and very old cricket ground. The Vine, it was called. They had watched over the town for 85 years since they were planted to celebrate the coronation of King Edward VII in the year 1902.

Autumn had arrived with its shortening days and lengthening nights. It was October and a very wet October at that. Birds brought news to the trees from the low-lying countryside near the town; they told them about the floods when the River Eden burst its banks and how sheep in the fields had to be rescued by the farmer in a boat.

The trees were worried by this news but it had happened before. They had weathered many storms in their lifetime; they had seen great snowfalls when they were clothed in a mantle of frosty white for many weeks; they had experienced droughts which had lasted so long that they feared they would shrivel up and die for lack of water.

Today, there was a different feeling in the air. The birds carried whisperings of a great storm gathering its strength away in the sea to the west, and as the wind began to rise and their leaves rustled gently together the oak trees talked fearfully to each other.

King Oak, the wisest of the oak trees, the fount of all knowledge, told his brothers and sisters that they must prepare for a night which would test their strength to the

"The birds carried whisperings of a great storm".

limit. ''Twist your roots into the ground'', he said, ''and bend with the wind.'' ''Yes, King Oak'', they said. ''Yes, we will. Just tell us what to do and we will trust in you as we always have.''

''Then listen carefully'', said King Oak. ''When the wind starts to blow we will tell stories to keep our courage up. We will each tell the others of the things we have seen in our lives that we remember most clearly.

It was late evening now and the wind had begun to whistle menacingly. ''May I start by telling you my story'', asked the Tree of Sorrow, already worried. ''Yes, please do'', said the others and as she began her tale the wind rose higher as if trying to blow the words away.

''I have remembered the sorrow of two terrible world wars'', she said. ''I have heard the distant thunder of cannon fire echoing across to England from the battlefields of Flanders. I have seen the character of Sevenoaks changed by war with young men and women marching around in khaki uniforms and I have seen guns trundle through the town. In the second war I remember bombs falling, and searchlights, and aeroplanes fighting in the sky above.

The other trees listened intently trying to forget the howling wind around them. The Tree of Sorrow continued her story. ''I have seen mothers say goodbye to their sons and girls kiss their sweethearts farewell under the shadow of my branches. I know the hatred that is about when men fight each other and the dreadful grief of women when their loved ones fail to return ...''

"I have seen the character of Sevenoaks changed by war".

"In the second war I remember bombs falling, and searchlights . . .

. . . and aeroplanes fighting in the sky above."

As her words faded into the night her sister oak, the Tree of Joy and Peace spoke up against the noise of the wind. "Don't tell us of such gloomy things", she said. "I will describe what I remember best." Her branches vibrated with excitement.

"I remember how men and women worked happily together in those difficult times, knowing their children would be grateful to them for ever. They were glad to be involved in a great and noble struggle, and I remember the outburst of joy and the celebrations at the end of both wars. The memorial to those heroes stands right here before us. Every year I look forward to the people of Sevenoaks standing among us to remember them."

The Tree of Joy and Peace continued. "I also recall the laughter and dancing in the streets, the excitement and happiness which gripped every heart when we celebrated three more coronations."

"Yes, yes", cried the oaks. "That's better, those are good memories."

As the cruel wind started to batter them the hour of midnight was passed and the oak who was known as the Tree of Music took on the task of keeping their spirits up.

"Do you recall some of the tunes we have heard the town band play", he asked, "and have you noticed how the styles have changed. Can any of you hum the songs of the music halls for instance. There was a great music hall in the Vine Gardens", he recalled sadly. "That was destroyed by a bomb."

"The memorial to those heroes stands right here before us."

"Oh yes", said the trees. "Oh yes. We remember the tunes", and their leaves rustled with melody. In the lull between the buffeting of the wind they sang right to the tips of their branches. They sang ballads and they crooned. They thought of jazz and they started to swing. They rocked and they rolled and they harmonised. "That's it", said the Tree of Music. "That's it", but the roar of the wind grew even stronger and drowned his voice.

"Hold firm", commanded King Oak. "Twist your roots into the ground. Slacken your branches. Let go of your leaves." The trees did their best to follow his advice; they bent with the wind but they still felt it tearing at their branches.

"Listen to me", said King Oak. "Have courage and do not fear. We must tell our stories", and he looked at the Tree of Sport who was usually a jolly fellow and eager for his turn. "What can you tell us?", he asked.

"I have seen a thing or two worth the memory", replied the Tree of Sport. "Great cricketers have come to play before us, stylish, elegant batsmen, bowlers who were wizards with the ball. Do you know our grandfather told me that the first century ever was scored on this old ground and in the same match they used three stumps instead of two for the very first time". The Tree of Sport paused to catch his breath. "This was because the best bowler of the day, Mr Lumpy Stevens who worked for Lord Sackville at Knole, over there, used to bowl a ball right between the two stumps and still not get a man out"

"On this old ground they used three stumps instead of two for the very first time."

"Well, well", said the other oak trees. "How interesting", and for the moment he had distracted them from the danger of the wind.

"Yes", said the Tree of Sport. "We have watched the young men of Sevenoaks learning this great game and then leaving us to play for the county of Kent. The very best have won a place in the England team. Oh, there's glory for you".

For a moment he was lost in happy memories. "Years ago whole families used to picnic in the shade of my branches, and the children would play games of their own, while their parents watched the cricket.

In that great park of Knole where so many of our cousins live in stately splendour, men and women have enjoyed the game of golf. Oh, I love a good game", said the Tree of Sport.

As he spoke the great warm wind hurled itself at his branches with added intensity and took his breath away. The trees shuddered as they felt their roots lifting in the soft soil; it was a strange and frightening feeling they had never experienced before.

They could hear distant cries as other trees had limbs ripped away. Their messengers, the birds, were nowhere to be seen; perhaps they were lucky, sheltering low down in the safety of thick hedges. If not they would have been caught by the wind and tossed into the darkness of the night.

King Oak sensed their alarm and he called to the Tree of Invention. "Take a good hold with your roots", he said, "and talk. Tell us about those amazing machines you have seen".

"Families used to picnic in the shade of my branches".

Slowly, very slowly and with great determination, to prevent his voice shaking with fear, the Tree of Invention began . ''I remember the first motor car in Sevenoaks'', he said, ''and what a stir it made. It belonged to a local doctor and it could do the work of two horses with ease; do you know one of the first fatal accidents with a motor car happened on this very road going down to the station''. As he spoke he became so involved in his story he quite forgot how frightened he was.

''Oh those trains. Do you know, when we were just seedlings, steam trains would stop at the station and whistle and toot, and the gentlemen of the town would leave their houses and go down to the station where the train was waiting for them. Can you believe that now—everything was so much more leisurely in those days.''

The Tree of Invention sighed but it was barely audible against the noise of the storm. ''I wish we still had those old steam engines'', he said. ''I wish we had the old station where there was a fire in the waiting room to warm the travellers and I wish the old cars would return. Today they all look the same to me.''

The other trees tried to show enthusiasm but now the night sky was dark no longer. It was illuminated, as if by lightning, on every side. ''What is happening'', cried the trees, ''We have never seen lightning so widespread as this before?''.

"I remember the first motor car in Sevenoaks".

"I fear", said the Tree of Invention. "I fear that the flashes are caused by power cables being brought to the ground . . ." He hesitated and a great chilling fear came to them all. It must be their friends and relatives, the great trees of England that were bringing the cables down as they fell. They stood in shocked silence for a moment, listening for the far-off cries.

Then the sixth tree, the Tree of Love and Creation stepped in, attempting to distract them with her story. "Artists have painted beautiful pictures here", she said, "when the scene was more peaceful . . ." but as she began to speak, her sister, The Tree of Sorrow, shrieked as she lost her hold on the ground and with a terrible cry she fell. "Help, help", she cried and her brothers and sisters leaned towards her, reaching out to help her, trying to stretch their boughs to hold her, but it was to no avail, they could not save her.

The storm thundered on; it was like an express train now. In the distance they could hear it coming, gathering strength, gathering speed, gathering anger until the great roar broke over and around everything that stood in its path.

King Oak shouted above the roar, urging the five others to cling on, to hold firm with their roots. "I can't", cried the Tree of Joy and Peace. "The soil is too wet, it will not hold me". With a cry of anguish which pierced the air above the howling of the wind, she fell too, and her roots pointed upwards towards the dark sky.

Seeing her sisters lying helpless before her, the Tree of Love and Creation knew how important it was for her to

*"She fell too and her roots pointed upwards towards
the sky."*

complete her story while they could still hear her, and she struggled to suppress her tears.

"Before our time great writers lived in Sevenoaks", she said, her voice creaking with emotion. "Jane Austen lived in the Red House and Charles Dickens came here too. H. G. Wells wrote the Time Machine in a house up the road."

Barely had she begun to speak when another savage attack was launched by the wind, which was now at its zenith and nearing 100 miles an hour—a hurricane force wind. The Tree of Music cried to King Oak. "It's no good, my leaves are too heavy, the soil is too wet, the wind is too strong", and he began to sing a long last lament as he fell slowly to the ground.

The keening and the wailing and the sad singing of the dying trees filled the air. "Brothers, sisters, do not despair", cried the Tree of Love and Creation. "I have watched young birds hatch from eggs in the nests in my branches and grow so quickly to learn to fly. The children of Sevenoaks have also grown quickly", she said. "I have seen two, three and sometimes four generations from the same family playing on the Vine, don't you see? . . ." but she was interrupted again.

"I can't fight the wind any more", cried the Tree of Sport desperately, and down, down, down, he went.

"Oh, do hold on, hold firm", King Oak pleaded to his remaining brother and sister, but even as he uttered the

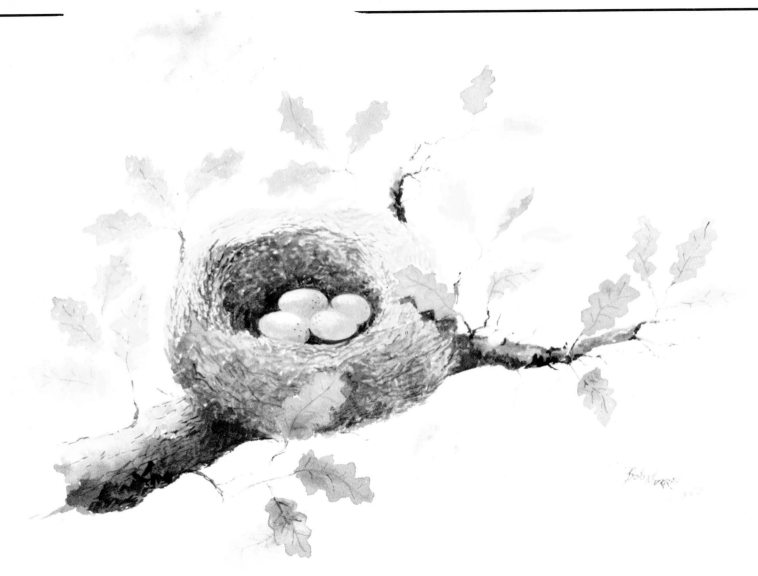

"I have seen birds hatch from eggs in the nests in my branches".

words the Tree of Invention was leaning and swaying and groaning and seconds later he too lost his hold.

"I must finish my story. I must", said the Tree of Love and Creation. "I know the power of life and love is all around us. I know that our acorns will fall into this wet earth and they will send up new shoots to become young oaks, just like us. I know, I know this will be. It is our comfort now. We shall live again". At this moment a massive blast wrapped itself around her trunk, twisted her out of the ground and threw her down beside the other five oaks.

King Oak stood alone in the dark night, using his wisdom and skill to resist the wiles of the wind, twisting his roots deeper still into the ground. He was resolute. "I will not go down", he said. "I will not let go. I will not give in to any hurricane. I must remain to guard the town of Sevenoaks".

All through the rest of the night the wind was locked in battle with King Oak, attacking him on all sides with its fury until, finally, as the dreadful night began to lose its darkness, the wind lessened and King Oak realised he had won the great battle for survival.

He stood alone, King Oak, Great Oak . . . One Oak, and huge tears flowed down his branches as he grieved for the six who had fallen.

As dawn began to break he prepared to meet the people of the town as they started to emerge from their houses.

Shocked and disbelieving they surveyed the wreckage of the night and, as they came to the Vine to see the fallen

"King Oak realised he had won the great battle for survival."

trees, they touched King Oak and he felt their warmth and affection flowing to him, and he was comforted.

That morning the whole world heard the story of the seven oaks as news of the terrible ''hurricane'' which had hit south-east England was flashed across the world by radio and television, for they had symbolised the destruction that had occurred in every town and village. Sevenoaks was One oak, One oak was King Oak and King Oak was famous.

Now the wise councillors of Sevenoaks knew the importance of the trees and when soldiers came to take them away, King Oak asked the birds to find out what would happen to them. The birds brought back the good news that they would not be burnt like other trees or turned into pulp. Their wood was to be used for furniture and souvenirs and even for fine panelling in the ceiling of a palace called Hampton Court, which had suffered a terrible fire. ''They will live again, indeed'', King Oak said to himself, recalling the words of The Tree of Love and Creation.

Soon a splendid fair was planned by the councillors for the replanting of seven, not six, young saplings around the Vine to give the town back the symbol of its name. King Oak rejoiced at the thought of welcoming his young relatives as he was rather lonely, even though so many people visited him now.

When the great day of the Hurricane Fair arrived at the beginning of December, 1987, there were balloons and kites and thousands of people came from all over the

"There were balloons and kites".

26

country to watch the replanting. Celebrities and local dignitaries and businessmen planted the new trees. Television cameras filmed the ceremony and there were stalls all over the Vine. A children's television programme called Blue Peter also provided another seven smaller saplings because children throughout the whole country had been so concerned, and they were planted in a group some way distant from the others.

For nearly a year King Oak enjoyed the company of the youngsters around him and he passed on the stories of the life of Sevenoaks that his brothers and sisters had told him, so that they would not be forgotten.

Sadly, there was a sickness abroad in England in those years; a sickness that gripped a few young men and twisted their minds to mindlessness. It warped their characters and turned them to acts of destruction and cruelty. It was called vandalism.

Exactly a year after the storm on the night of October 15, 1988, vandals came to Sevenoaks in the night, and King Oak suffered again. He watched in helpless rage as the thoughtless youths, showing the feebleness of their minds struck at his young friends. The young oaks were bent and broken and torn and once again King Oak grieved as he heard their agony. "Will it never end?" he cried.

"The young oaks were bent and broken and torn."

The day which followed should have been a happy celebration of the recovery from the storm, with the burying of a casket carrying mementoes of that day a year before, but it was not to be. Instead, there was shock and disbelief again. Once more Sevenoaks became ''One Oak'' and made the headlines for all the wrong reasons. This time the loss of the young symbolised the destruction that could be caused by man instead of nature.

A few weeks later young children, older children, handicapped children, children of all shapes and sizes came to The Vine to replant once again, shovelling, digging, having a wonderful time giving back to the town its name—only this time bigger, stronger trees were planted and surrounded with iron bars to protect them.

"Bigger, stronger trees were planted and surrounded with iron bars to protect them".

King Oak hoped upon hope that it would be the last time he would see the television cameras whirring in front of him. He had suffered enough. He wanted to enjoy his old age in serenity, remembering the stories of lost friends, keeping watch over the peaceful, sporting, musical, inventive, loving and, only occasionally, sorrowful town of Sevenoaks.

The seven oaks

Invention   Sorrow   Joy and Peace   Music   King Oak   Love and Creation   Sport

Other books from Froglets

In The Wake of the Hurricane (West Kent)
ISBN 0-9513019-0-X   £7.00

In The Wake of the Hurricane (National)
ISBN 0-9513019-1-8   £7.50

In The Wake of the Hurricane (National)
ISBN 0-9513019-4-2   (Hardback)   £11.95

Surrey in the Hurricane
ISBN 0-9513019-2-6   £7.50

Hurricane Gilbert
ISBN 0-9513019-5-0   £7.50

London's Hurricane
ISBN 0-9513019-3-4   (Paperback)   £7.95

London's Hurricane
ISBN 0-9513019-8-5   (Hardback)   £11.95

Eye on the Hurricane
ISBN 0-9513019-6-9   (Paperback)   £7.95
ISBN 0-9513019-7-7   (Hardback)   £11.95